A PET WHAT?!

MY PET SUGAR GLIDER

BY PAIGE V. POLINSKY

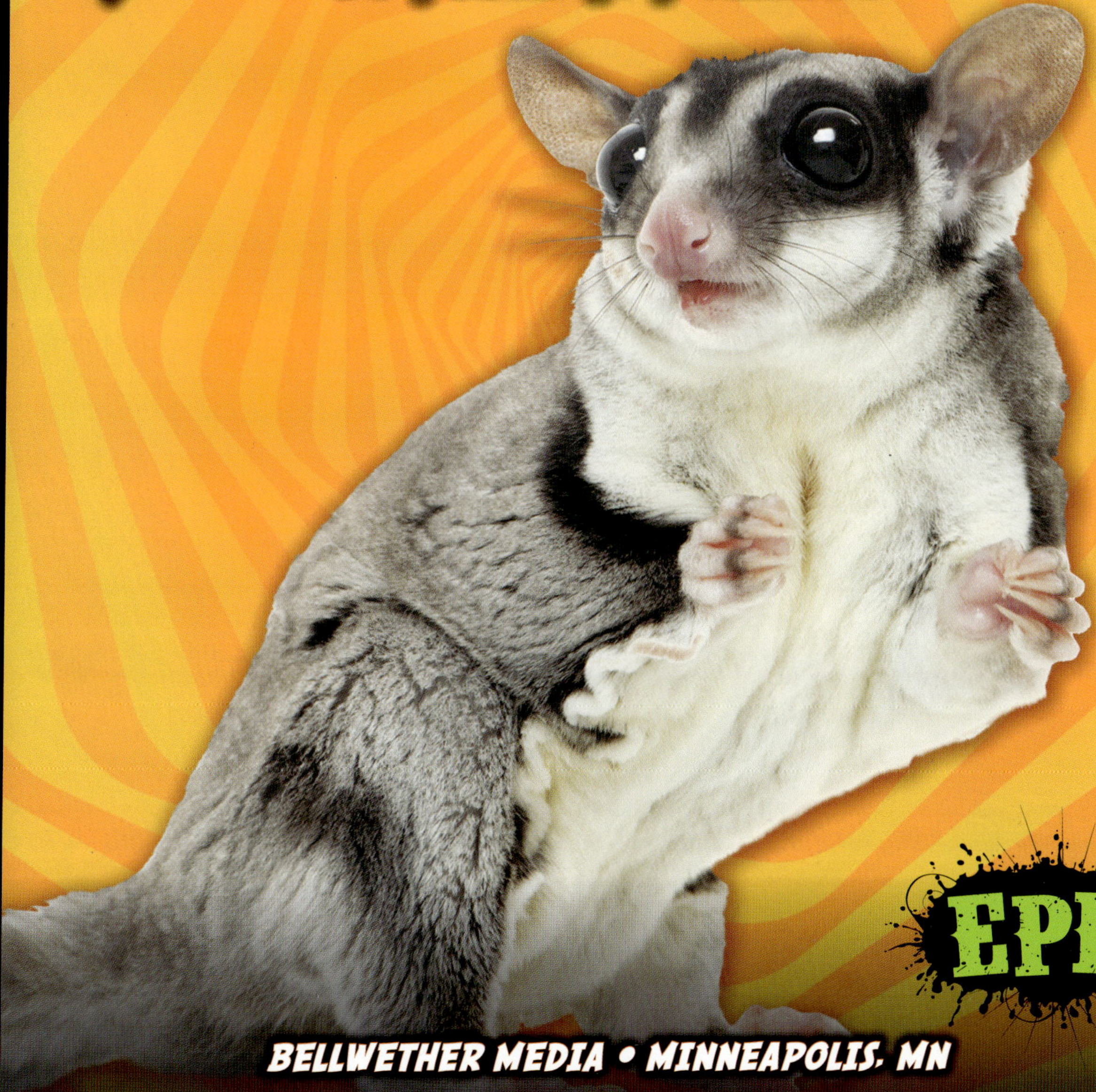

EPIC

BELLWETHER MEDIA • MINNEAPOLIS, MN

Action and adventure collide in EPIC. Plunge into a universe of powerful beasts, hair-raising tales, and high-speed excitement. Astonishing explorations await. Can you handle it?

This edition first published in 2020 by Bellwether Media, Inc.

Library of Congress Cataloging-in-Publication Data

Names: Polinsky, Paige V., author.
Title: My pet sugar glider / Paige V. Polinsky.
Description: Minneapolis, MN : Bellwether Media, 2020. | Series: A pet what?! | Includes bibliographical references and index. | Audience: Ages 7-12. | Audience: Grades 4-6. | Summary: "Engaging images accompany information about pet sugar gliders. The combination of high-interest subject matter and light text is intended for students in grades 2 through 7"– Provided by publisher.
Identifiers: LCCN 2019034559 (print) | LCCN 2019034560 (ebook) | ISBN 9781644871867 (library binding) | ISBN 9781618918666 (ebook)
Subjects: LCSH: Sugar gliders as pets–Juvenile literature. | Sugar glider–Juvenile literature. | Marsupials–Juvenile literature.
Classification: LCC SF459.S83 P65 2020 (print) | LCC SF459.S83 (ebook) | DDC 599.2/32–dc23
LC record available at https://lccn.loc.gov/2019034559
LC ebook record available at https://lccn.loc.gov/2019034560

Editor: Betsy Rathburn   Designer: Josh Brink

Printed in the United States of America, North Mankato, MN.

TABLE OF CONTENTS

POCKET PETS 4

BETTER IN PAIRS! 10

A SWEET CHALLENGE 16

GLOSSARY 22

TO LEARN MORE 23

INDEX 24

POCKET PETS

Two little sugar gliders leap from branch to branch. They bark and chirp with joy!

Sugar gliders are small **marsupials**. These cute **mammals** need lots of love and care!

Sugar gliders have soft gray fur. Their tails are long and bushy. Big eyes peek from their furry faces.

Sugar gliders have special skin flaps. They connect their wrists and back legs. The flaps help them sail through the air!

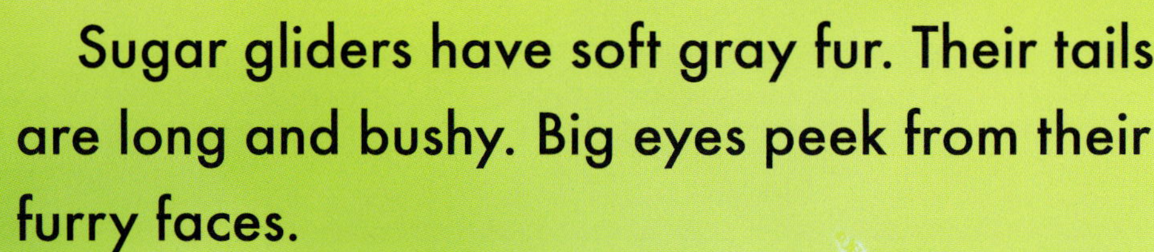

SUGAR GLIDER PROFILE

- **Animal Type:** mammal
- **Life Span:** up to 15 years
- **Length:** up to 8 inches (20 centimeters)
- **Weight:** up to 6 ounces (170 grams)

Wild gliders live in **Oceania** and Southeast Asia. Pet gliders are not fully **domesticated**. Some places ban them.

Gliders are too much work for some owners. **Rescues** help find the animals new homes.

BETTER IN PAIRS!

Lonely sugar gliders can grow very sick. They need to live with another glider.

Tall wire cages make good homes for these pets. High branches are perfect for playing!

SUGAR GLIDER CAGE

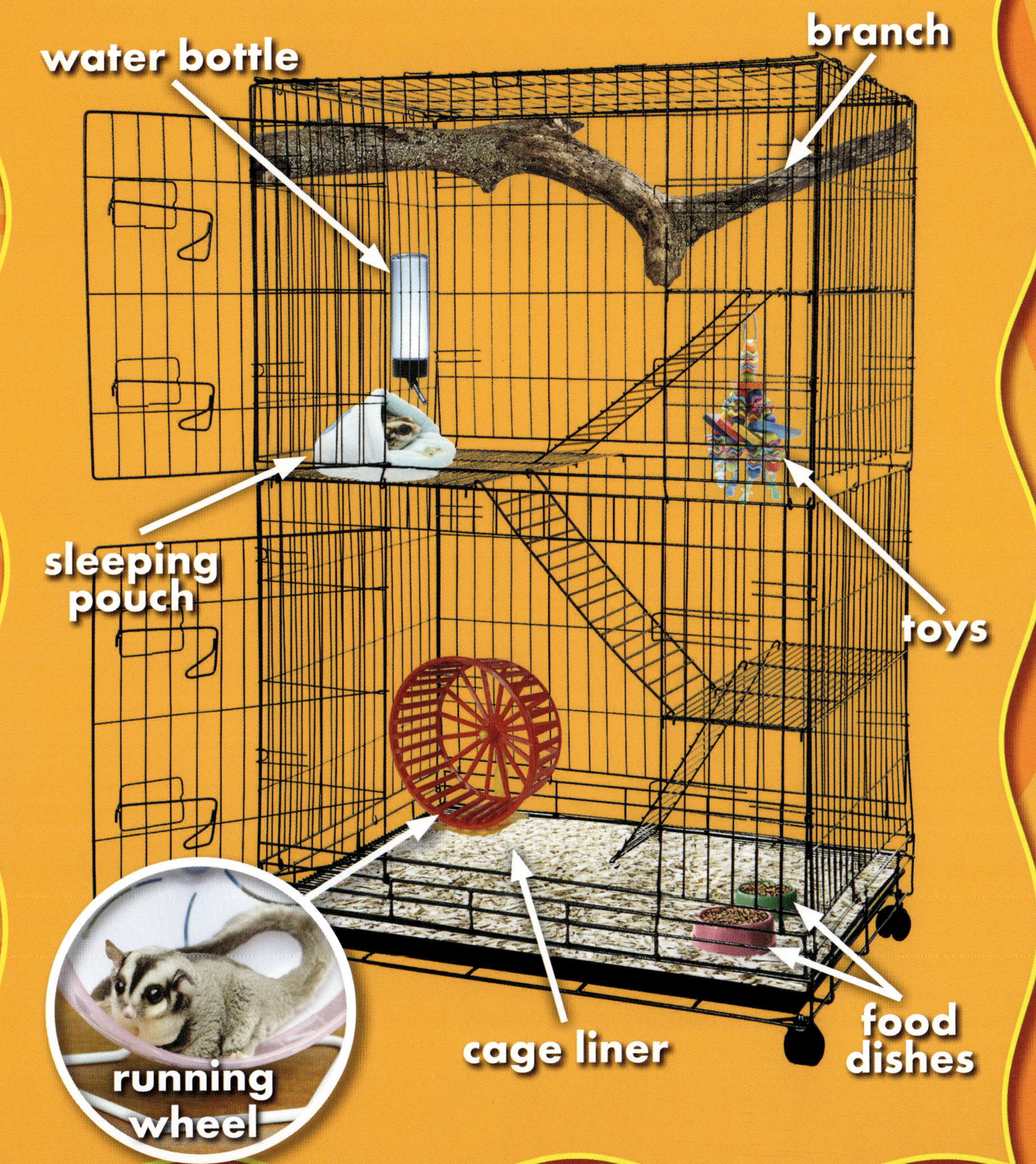

Sugar gliders like to live up high. Cloth pouches give them cozy spots to rest.

Pouch Parents

Female sugar gliders have a belly pouch. They raise their babies there!

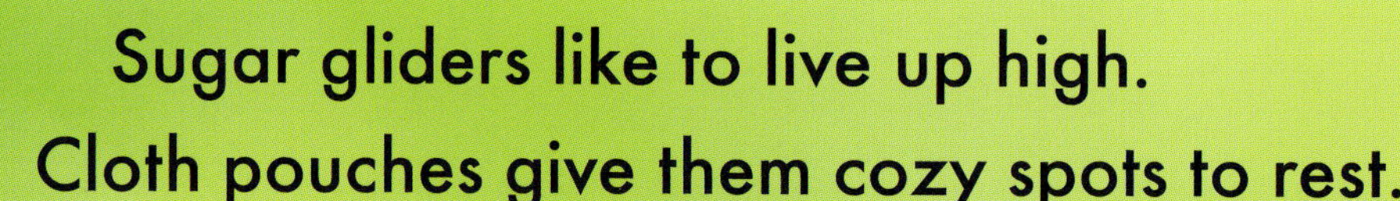

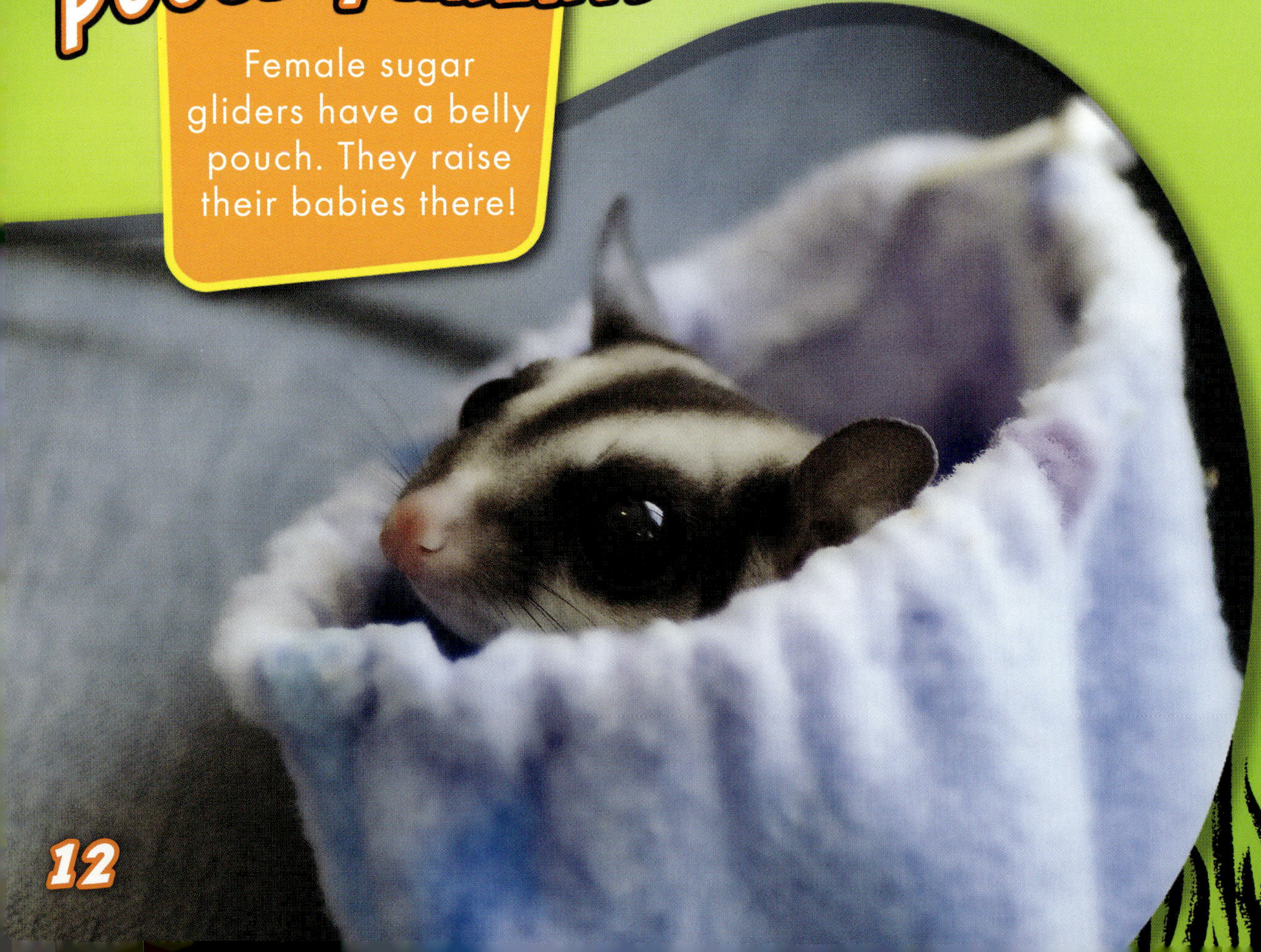

Cloth **liners** help keep cages tidy.
Owners should clean these every day.

Sugar gliders' dishes should always be full.
These pets eat **nectar** and leafy greens.
   They need live bugs and cooked meats, too.
Fresh fruit is a treat!

SUGAR GLIDER CARE DUTIES

Daily
- ☑ pick up waste from liners
- ☑ feed
- ☑ fill water dish
- ☑ play outside of cage

Weekly
- ☑ wash cage liners
- ☑ wash toys and dishes

Monthly
- ☑ scrub full cage
- ☑ trim nails

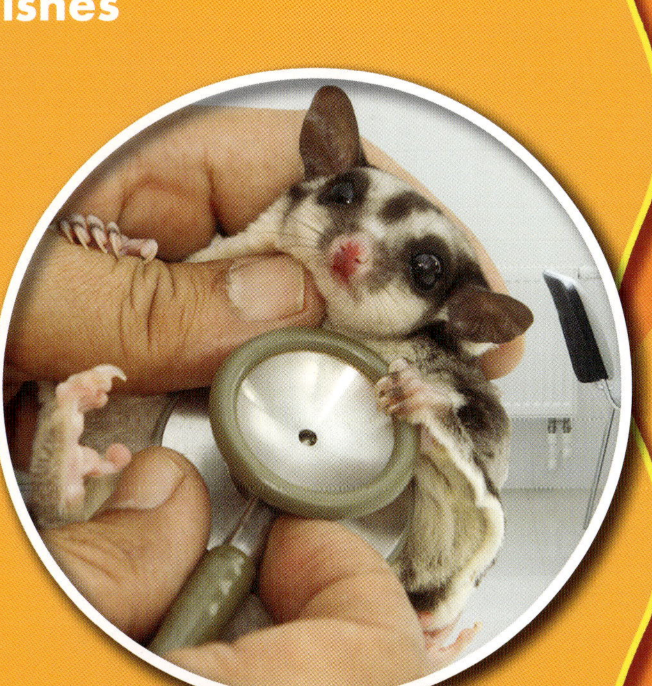

As Needed
- ☑ bring to vet

A SWEET CHALLENGE

Sugar gliders love sweet treats. But too much sugar can harm their teeth! Regular vet visits are important.

Gliders have sharp fingernails. Owners should trim them every month.

SUGAR GLIDER HEALTH SUPPLIES

another sugar glider

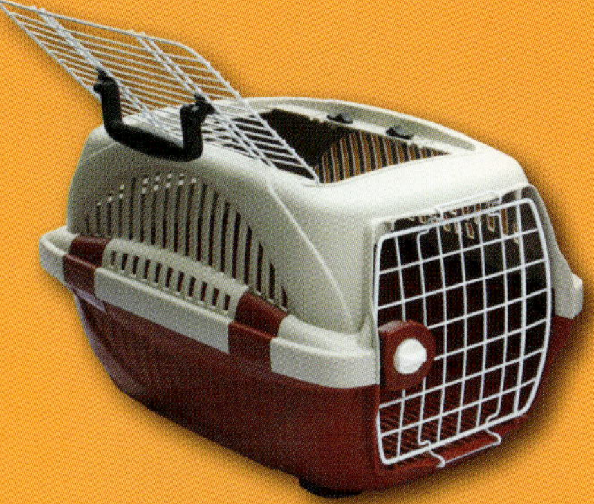

travel carrier for vet visits

toys for exercise

nail clippers

soft brush

Sugar gliders like to be held. But most gliders fear strangers. They may nip and scratch.

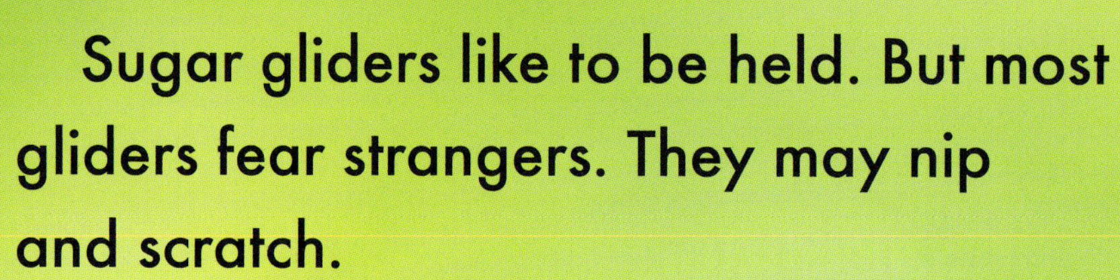

Sugar gliders sleep all day. They like to play
at night! Wooden toys and bird swings are fun.

Sugar gliders feel safest in high places. They like to ride in pouches or pockets.

Sugar gliders are not easy pets. But these cute critters can be wonderful friends!

GLOSSARY

domesticated—trained to need and accept the care of humans

liners—materials that go on the bottom of pet cages to keep them clean and comfortable

mammals—warm-blooded animals that have backbones and feed their young milk

marsupials—animals that carry their babies in a pocket of skin on the mother's stomach

nectar—a sweet liquid made by plants to attract animals

Oceania—an area of the central and southern Pacific Ocean that includes Australia, New Guinea, New Zealand, and many other islands

rescues—places from which people can adopt animals in need of homes

TO LEARN MORE

AT THE LIBRARY

Murray, Julie. *Sugar Gliders*. Minneapolis, Minn.: Abdo, 2018.

Polinsky, Paige V. *My Pet Ferret*. Minneapolis, Minn.: Bellwether Media, 2020.

Wilson, Paula M. *Sugar Gliders*. North Mankato, Minn.: Capstone Press, 2019.

ON THE WEB

FACTSURFER

Factsurfer.com gives you a safe, fun way to find more information.

1. Go to www.factsurfer.com.

2. Enter "sugar gliders" into the search box and click 🔍.

3. Select your book cover to see a list of related web sites.

INDEX

Asia, 8

babies, 12

branch, 4, 10

cages, 10, 11, 13

care duties, 15

domesticated, 8

eyes, 6

females, 12

fingernails, 16

food, 14

fur, 6

health supplies, 17

liners, 13

mammals, 5

marsupials, 5

nectar, 14

Oceania, 8

owners, 9, 13, 16, 19

playing, 10, 19

pouches, 12, 20

profile, 7

rescues, 9

skin flaps, 6

sleep, 19

sounds, 4, 19

strangers, 18

tails, 6

teeth, 16

toys, 19

treat, 14, 16

vet, 16

wild sugar gliders, 8